# PLANET EARTH
# GETS WELL

# Madeline Kaplan
## Illustrated by Taillefer Long

ISBN: 1-4196-8986-X
ISBN-13: 9781419689864

Visit www.booksurge.com to order additional copies.

# PLANET EARTH GETS WELL

## by Madeline Kaplan

FOR MATTHEW, BRETT AND MELANIE.
YOU ARE MY WORLD.

One day long ago, Planet Earth felt sick.

"What's wrong," said Earth's Mother.

"I don't know, Mother, but I think I have a runny nose. My ice caps are melting; and no matter what I do, I can't stop them from running into the ocean. I told a polar bear not to play too far away from its mother because I didn't want it to float away on a piece of ice and then have to swim home."

"Achew," sneezed Planet Earth. "I need another tissue, please."

"Let me feel your head," said Earth's Mother. "You feel warm to me. I warned you about your People wearing you out."

"But, Mother," Planet Earth cried, "I love my People. I want them to stay and play with me, so I let them do whatever they want."

"And that is the problem," Earth's Mother replied. "You think you are being your People's friend by letting them wear you out, but you are putting them at risk. The toys they are playing with are causing your temperature to rise. You are running a very high fever. If you don't allow yourself to get well, your People will also get sick, and then what fun will you have with each other?"

Planet Earth thought about this; but his temperature was so high, he just couldn't think straight. He was having trouble breathing.

Earth's Mother had trouble understanding him when he tried to speak. She caused a breeze to ripple through the trees, and Planet Earth felt cooler.

"Achew!" With all of his strength, he asked his mother what he should tell his People the next time they wanted to play with him.

"Tell them to please help to conserve your energy. They must understand that if they want to play with you, you must be strong and your fever must go down. Tell them that you try your best to stay healthy, but you need their help."

"But what should I ask them to do?" Planet Earth exclaimed. "Achew!" His head still hurt, and his throat was sore. "Mommy, I feel so warm!"

"You have a bad case of global warming," Earth's Mother replied, "and there is no vaccine for it. Your People are the only ones who can help bring your temperature down. Here are some things they can do to make you feel better."

Planet Earth held his head because he was feeling really grumpy. But he tried to pay attention to what his mother was telling him.

"Ask them to drive smaller cars that use less fuel. Fuel is like your blood. You need enough of it to run through your body or you will become weak."

"OK," said Planet Earth, "I will ask that they leave more of my fuel running through my body. When my People use too much fuel, I have trouble seeing because the fuel puts clouds of poisons in the air. Then my forests get brown and ugly. I think they are sick too."

"They are," Earth's Mother replied. "But they CAN get better. If your People put less pollution in the air, your forests will grow strong and green again, and your People will feel better too."

Planet Earth wanted the forests to be green and strong again. He would ask his People to use less fuel and to help him conserve his Energy. That didn't seem so hard!

"Good," said Earth's Mother. "Next, you can ask them to use the sun to heat their homes. The sun's warmth can heat their homes. That will leave more of your fuel for you so you can stay strong. That will help you feel better.

"But remember," Earth's Mother warned, "you still have a tear in the outer layer of your skin. Until that is completely healed, too much sun can harm your People. So tell them to use the sun's energy wisely but not to stay out in the sun long without covering up. When you are completely well, the sun will be less harmful to them."

"I understand," said Planet Earth. "The sun's energy is good for us, but all the harmful pollution in the air caused my temperature to go up, and that burned a hole in my ozone layer. My ozone layer is like my skin—right, Mom?"

"That's right," said Earth's Mother. "Your ozone layer is like your skin. It protects you and your People from the sun's harmful rays. Until your ozone layer is completely healed, you must tell your People to wear sunscreen when they play on the beach.

"Are you feeling better yet?"

SUNBLOCK

"A little," said Planet Earth, "but I know it will take me a long time to be well enough to go out and play again. Sometimes, I feel too hot, and sometimes I feel too cold. And sometimes big storms make me lose my balance and I feel really yucky."

"That's because when you have a temperature, you are not able to keep your balance and your stomach gets upset. That's when it rains and snows a lot. And sometimes you feel so off-balance, a hurricane will keep you in bed for days," Earth's Mother explained.

"Achew! Oh my," Planet Earth cried. "I don't like feeling yucky. I have to get my People to help keep me in balance."

"You can," Earth's Mother said. "There are so many other ways they can help you get well."

"I know," Planet Earth exclaimed. He was so excited, his clouds bumped together and made the thunder start to go BOOM!

"Oops!" Planet Earth cried. "I didn't mean to get so excited."

"That's okay," Earth's Mother replied. "Until you're feeling better, you must try to stay still so that Nature understands that it is safe to keep living with you."

"You can do that by reminding your people to always THINK GREEN. That means that they are thinking about Nature and how to keep it safe.

"Nature takes care of all of the animals that live with you, Planet Earth, and all of the flowers and plants and the food that your People eat. Nature is everywhere, in the ocean and on land, with all the living things that need to stay healthy like you do."

Although Planet Earth understood what his mother was telling him, he just couldn't stop coughing. It took him a minute to catch his breath. His nose was still stuffy, and his head still hurt. But he knew that his mother was right.

"So THINKING GREEN will help me get well?" Planet Earth asked. "And if I stay well, then all living things will stay well, too?"

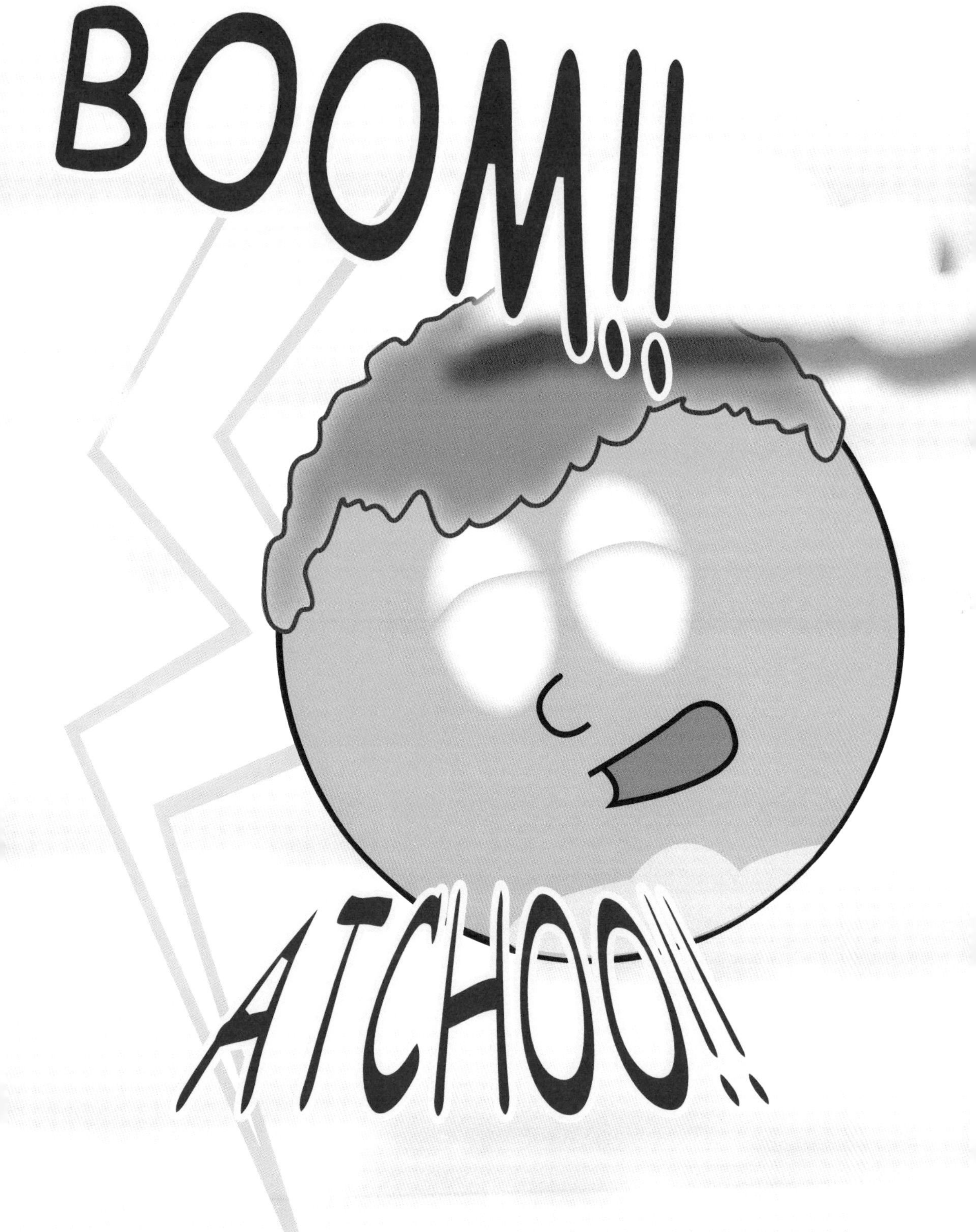
BOOM!!
ATCHOO!!

"Exactly, replied Earth's Mother. "All of your people and all of Nature, the animals that live on you and the fish that swim in your oceans, will stay healthy and strong. THINKING GREEN is your daily vitamin. If everyone gives you your "GREEN" vitamin, then you will stay healthy and strong for your People."

"Mom, please ask my People to come to my next birthday party, and tell them that my favorite color is GREEN! Tell them I don't need any new toys unless they can be recycled. And ask them to walk to our house or have their moms arrange carpools to help save fuel!"

Planet Earth was amazed at what his mother had told him. It was so easy to remember. People could help make him well by doing such little things. They could save trees in the forest by using less paper. They could help him to breathe better by recycling and using less plastic. They could drive smaller cars to leave more fuel for his muscles. They could use the sun's heat instead of oil to warm their homes. There was lots they could do to make Planet Earth feel better. And he was sure that his People loved him enough to help save his energy and make him well again.

**THE END**

982183